E

Bunting, Eve
The spook Birds

THE SPOOK BIRDS

THE SPOOK BIRDS

Eve Bunting
Illustrations by Blanche Sims

ALBERT WHITMAN & COMPANY, CHICAGO

Text © 1981 by Eve Bunting
Illustrations © 1981 by Albert Whitman & Company
Printed simultaneously in Canada by
General Publishing, Limited, Toronto
All rights reserved. Printed in U.S.A.

Library of Congress Cataloging in Publication Data

Bunting, Eve, 1928-
  The spook birds.

  SUMMARY: Larry witnesses some mysterious goings-on
at his rich grandmother's house when the stuffed birds
in her glass case suddenly come alive.
  [1. Mystery and detective stories] I. Sims, Blanche.
II. Title.
PZ7.B91527Som   [Fic]   81-686
ISBN 0-8075-7587-9 (lib. bdg.)   AACR2

To Des, Andrea, and Michelle with love.

Chapter One

I spend a week each summer at Grandmother's. And I really like it. Except for old Rub-a-dub, Gram's housekeeper. She's a mean old coot. Always picking up. Always rub-a-dubbing. Always hassling me. I don't think she likes boys my age. Or boys any age.

But when I went into Gram's dining room for the first time this visit, I saw something else I didn't like. A glass case filled with birds hung on the wall.

The birds were dead. Stuffed. They were propped on twigs. I guess that was to fool you into thinking that they were still alive.

It was spooky. Once those birds had flown and sung. They'd been free. Then someone

had caught them. Someone had scooped out
their insides and stuffed them. Ugh!

"Creepy, huh?" a voice asked. "Some
people might think they're pretty. I think
they're awful."

I spun around. It was Jill.

Jill lives in the house next door. She's one
of the best things about coming to Gram's.
Jill's my age. And she's just like a boy.

I hadn't seen her for a whole year. And had
she changed! For one thing, her hair was
long now. I mean, mine's long, too. But hers
was middle-of-the-back long. And not
stringy.

"Hi," I said. My spooky feeling had gone. I
felt a bit shy.

"Those birds have been dead for more than
ten years," Jill said. "They used to be in
your grandfather's club, but it's being torn
down. I guess he really liked the birds. So
your Gram saved them. She had someone
bring them here last week."

I sure wished she hadn't. I looked at those birds. There was a big, black one in the middle with shiny, black eyes. It seemed as if that bird was looking right back at me. I moved and the eyes seemed to follow me.

I swallowed. It was silly to feel creepy. There was probably something about the light that made the eyes look funny. The bird was dead. They were all dead.

Chapter Two

Jill pointed at the case. "The big black one in the middle is a crow. The two yellow ones are finches. That's a robin. The guy with the long beak is a woodpecker. I don't know about the others."

I nodded. There were thirteen stuffed birds. And it wasn't even Thanksgiving. The crow was the biggest.

I looked again, and my heart just about stopped beating. One of the crow's eyes was closed now. I knew that just a second ago both eyes had been open.

A face floated in the glass. I almost jumped out of my skin.

It was Rub-a-dub. I hadn't heard her come up behind us. "So here you are, Master Larry," she said.

Rub-a-dub is always slipping around, watching. You can't hear her because she wears tennies. The old kind that lace high.

Rub-a-dub is scared to death you might mess up her house. When I was little she was always after me. There was no way to get a frog past Rub-a-dub. She didn't even like a clean worm in a clean jar.

She wiped a cloth over the glass of the case. Rub-a-dub always carries a cloth up her sleeve. I used to think it was for nose blowing. But it isn't.

"Dirty!" Rub-a-dub said. "And the case is sealed. I need to clean the glass inside. Twenty years of dust—that's what's in there."

I looked at Jill. She gave a little snore.

That's her way of hiding a laugh. I didn't feel shy anymore. She was just the same Jill, even with long hair. I rolled my eyes to make her snore more.

"It looks real clean inside to me," I told Rub-a-dub.

Rub-a-dub sniffed. "I'd like to vacuum those dusty feathers."

I thought of her vacuum. Would it feel like wind to the birds? How could it? They were dead.

Suddenly I felt goose bumps all along my arms. I looked at the crow.

No wonder I had goose bumps! Now *both* its shiny eyes were tightly closed.

Chapter Three

Jill went home before Gram came back.

Gram's great. She's over seventy, but you'd never know it. She'd been out jogging. Her jogging suit was Santa Claus red.

"How did you get here so fast, love?" she asked.

"I took an early bus."

She hugged me tightly. She smelled of jogging sweat and roses. She smelled rich, which she is.

We aren't rich at all. Dad's a painter. A picture painter, I mean, not a house painter, though he says he'd make more money at that. Gram keeps trying to give us money. She says she has loads. But Dad won't take it. I don't mind our kind of poor. But Gram's kind of rich is nice, too.

At Gram's we have steak for dinner. Or prime rib. Stuff like that. Rub-a-dub changes out of her tennies and puts on a black dress. She slinks behind us with the dishes. We always have candles and napkins at home, too, of course. But our napkins are the kind made out of dimpled paper.

Tonight Gram and I had lobster in some kind of sauce.

The birds were on the wall behind me. Their eyes watched my back. I could feel them. I slid down in my seat. I wanted to look and see if the crow's eyes were open or closed. But my head wouldn't turn around. My head had more sense than I had.

Gram carried her coffee cup over to the bird cage. She tapped on the glass.

"They're not alive," I said quickly. "They

can't hear you." I made myself look at the crow. Its eyes were still closed.

Gram smiled. "I know. They're all dead as dodos. I don't like them that much. But your Grandpa did. When I took the birds it was for him, you know?"

I knew. I thought it was nice of her to have those dead things around just because Gramps liked them.

A wire ran from the case to an electric socket.

"What's that for?" I asked.

"The club people say it keeps the air in the case fresh."

"But wasn't the case unplugged to bring it here?"

Gram nodded. "For a half hour or so, I suppose. It didn't seem to do the birds any harm."

"How could it?" I asked. "Dead birds don't care if the air is fresh."

"I know." Gram smiled again. "You want

to hear something crazy? I thought I saw the robin's wings flutter once. It was just as the man was setting up the case. I told him, and he laughed. He said it was only the movement of the case. And of course that's what it was." She tapped the glass again. "I don't understand why the case has to be plugged in. Maybe it's to keep bugs away. After all, the birds are dead. And bugs get onto dead things."

Ugh again! I looked at the birds and shivered.

Chapter Four

Jill and I walked to my grandfather's club the next day. She was wearing a blue T-shirt. It was the same color as her eyes. Last year I didn't notice her eyes. Maybe they weren't that blue last year.

The club was half knocked down. There was a big crane on the road. An iron ball swung and smashed, and more of the walls fell.

Mr. Kidd stood on the sidewalk. He's someone big in the club. He and Grandpa used to play chess together. Sometimes he still comes to dinner at Gram's.

Each time the ball hit the wall of the building, Mr. Kidd closed his eyes. "The club's opening again," he said. "But in a new place. It won't be the same."

"I suppose you know Gram took the birds," I said. "The ones that Grandpa liked. Who . . . who stuffed those birds, Mr. Kidd?"

"That was old Bill Bedder," Mr. Kidd said. "He was the caretaker at the club. He passed away about ten years ago. Bill loved the birds. He used to whistle to them. He had names for all of them. The big crow was Clem, I remember. He'd whistle 'Darling Clementine.' He acted as if those birds were alive. It's a good thing old Bill doesn't know his birds have gone from the club." Mr. Kidd's voice was low. "But maybe he does know."

"What do you mean?" I asked. "If he . . . passed away . . . how could he know?"

"It was silly of me to say that." Mr. Kidd looked ashamed. "It's just that people have been whispering. They say old Bill's ghost wanders around the club. They say they still hear him whistling. It's all nonsense, of course."

"Of course." I wondered if the crow's eyes opened when Bill whistled. I wondered if the robin fluttered. But, of course, that was nonsense, too. Bill Bedder and the birds were all dead.

"How did Mr. Bedder know how to stuff birds?" Jill asked. "That must be hard to do."

"Bill wasn't always the club caretaker. He had been a scientist once. Maybe he learned then. I heard Bill had a lot of newfangled ideas. Other scientists didn't always go along with him."

"He sure was a good bird stuffer," Jill said. "You'd swear those birds were still alive. If you didn't know better."

"You sure would," I said. "If you didn't know better."

Chapter Five

I couldn't sleep that night. The birds flew
and fluttered inside my head. Bill Bedder
had been dead for ten years. The birds must
have been dead longer than that. Ten years!
I didn't even know if birds lived ten years.
Butterflies died in a couple of days. And
those birds had no food. No water. No air.
Unless the wire brought in air. But for
what? Nothing could live for ten years
without water or food.

I tossed and tumbled. I decided I must be
hungry. What I needed was a munch.
Rub-a-dub might be a mean old bird. But she
kept a well-stuffed refrigerator. Bird!
Stuffed! I had stuffed birds on the brain.

My clock said midnight. Witches' hour.
Ghost time. Baloney, I told myself. Snack
time.

I took my flashlight. No need to waken
Gram or Rub-a-dub with lights. Rub-a-dub
would only creep after me to sweep up my
crumbs.

The kitchen was to the left. The dining
room was to the right. I started for the
kitchen, but my feet turned right.

I shone the flashlight into the case. It
gleamed on the birds' eyes. They were sharp

and bright and watchful. All except the crow's. They were still closed.

I had figured out how that had happened. The glue, or whatever held the eyes open, probably had come unstuck. After all, the case had been moved. The crow'd been jolted. Nothing to sweat about.

The birds were all in their right places. So? What had I expected? Spooky doings at the stroke of midnight?

I headed for the kitchen, and I didn't look over my shoulder once.

I got milk and bread and pâté, which is this paste stuff that Rub-a-dub makes. It looks awful, but it tastes great.

I was halfway back upstairs when I heard the whistling.

You think hair can't stand on end? It can.

Somewhere, soft as a breeze, someone was whistling "Darling Clementine."

Chapter Six

Gram took me shopping the next morning. She always loads me up with stuff. Mostly it's too fancy. But if my way of life ever changes to be full-on first class, I'll be ready.

We had lunch in a place with waiters. The head one bowed and gave Gram a rose. I never saw a dumber looking guy.

"Did you hear anything last night?" I asked Gram.

Gram cocked her head at me and nodded.

My heart lurched. Then she'd heard the whistling, too.

She took a small bite of her crab cocktail.

I waited till she swallowed. "What did you hear?"

"My grandson having a midnight snack."
Gram grinned. "I almost came downstairs,
too. But I have to watch my figure. If I don't,
no one else will."

"Did you hear . . . whistling?" I asked.

Gram grinned. "That's Rub-a-dub. She
whistles and puffs and snores all night long.
That woman sleeps like a zombie. I wonder
how she doesn't wake herself up."

No way that whistler was Rub-a-dub, I
thought. Nobody sleep-whistles a tune.

In the afternoon Jill and I swam in her
pool. Jill's rich, too, and her long hair is pale
yellow. I didn't notice that last year, either.
Man, last year I sure didn't see much!

I told her about last night. "Maybe I
imagined it," I said. "I imagine a lot of
things."

Jill sat on her towel. "You know what I
think?" she asked. "I think we should open
up that case and take a look at those birds
close up."

I thought about it. "We'd have to be careful. That case must be as old as the birds. We don't want to break the glass."

"Let's try." Jill began to get up.

"Wait a sec. Rub-a-dub will catch us. She catches everything." I stood up. "I'll go see if the coast is clear. If it is, I'll call you."

I ran back to Gram's and peeked into the dining room. For once, Rub-a-dub wasn't around. I carried a chair across to the case and climbed up.

And I saw something weird. The top was just sitting on loose. Bits of putty lay on the carpet. Someone else had had Jill's idea. And not too long ago. Crumbs of any kind don't lie long on Rub-a-dub's rug.

I swallowed. The case was open. All I had to do was lift off the top.

Chapter Seven

I got down from the chair. My knees felt
weak. I stared through the glass at the birds.
And suddenly one of the finches fell.

I swear, I jumped back six feet.

The finch lay at the bottom of the case. Its
legs stuck up. Its claws were crooked. A
yellow feather drifted in the air.

I was so scared I couldn't breathe.
Somehow, all the birds looked blurred—as if
they were in a fog. I blinked. The mist was
still there. It was on the glass. I reached out
and wiped it. But the blurring was on the
inside. A drop of water trickled down. The
case was like a car with the windows
shut—a car full of live, breathing people.

I really wanted to take that lid off. But I was frightened. Frightened of a bunch of dead birds. Besides, I thought, Jill should be here. Fair is fair. This was her idea.

I called her, and she came over right away.

We stood, peering in at the finch. Then I stood on the chair. I lifted off the lid and passed it to Jill.

There was a kind of humming sound, the sound a refrigerator makes. Coldness wafted up around my face. It was like a tomb in that case. I reached down. My hand knocked the crow off its perch. It fell with a crash. I grabbed for the finch. And I tell you, my stomach heaved.

A stuffed bird should be hard and stiff, right? This one was cold and clammy. And wet.

Chapter Eight

I set the finch on the chair.

Jill bent over it. "It doesn't look that dead," she said.

"I hope I look as good when I've been gone for more than ten years." I was trying to show how cool I was. But my insides felt as clammy as the bird's.

"Get that dirty thing off my chair!" Rub-a-dub had sneaked up behind us in her trusty tennies. She had a broom, a dust pan, and her rag. "Get it off," she said again.

I slid the finch onto a copy of *House Beautiful*. It slithered around. So did my stomach.

Rub-a-dub began cleaning up the putty
crumbs. Then she stood on the chair. She
wiped the mist from the inside of the glass.
A blue bird fell.

"Master Larry, set that one back up," she
ordered. "And the black one. And the yellow
one you took out."

"Did you take the top off?" Jill asked her.

"Yes. Anything that comes into this house has to be cleaned. Tomorrow Master Larry can nail it back on."

She would have made a great Hitler, old Rub-a-dub. I picked up the finch. I tried to set it on the branch but it fell off again. I wiped my hands on my jeans.

"The birds need to be wired on," Rub-a-dub said. "You can do that tomorrow, too, Master Larry. Set the top on for now. Then go wash up for supper."

She still talks to me like I'm five years old. I wish she'd quit. Especially in front of Jill.

I sneaked a look at the crow.

Its eyes were open again, watching me.

No, that was dumb. That bird couldn't be watching me. It must have had another jolt, that was all. Maybe when Rub-a-dub took the top off. So the eyes had moved again.

My hands were shaky as I set the lid back on. I was careful to leave a crack so the birds

could breathe. Breathe? I was going bonkers.
Dead birds don't need to breathe.

Chapter Nine

Things kept waking me in the night. I thought I heard a crash. I thought I heard birds chirping. As I told Jill, I have a big imagination.

I wakened at dawn and watched my room fill with light. I didn't want to go downstairs. I didn't want to look in the dining room. But some force seemed to pull me.

I went slowly down the stairs.

The birds were out.

They filled the dining room. Their wings beat at the air. They smashed against the windows. They clung to the tops of the pictures. They thumped against the walls and fell, dazed, on the rug.

The glass lid lay in a hundred pieces on the floor.

I imagined the birds in the night, rising, pushing. The lid had toppled and they'd rushed out.

I don't know how long I stood, my arms shielding my head from the whip of their wings. Then I ran to the windows and flung them open.

The crow led the way to freedom. The other birds swooped behind him. I felt their joy in all of my bones. I seemed to rise with them.

They circled against the morning sky over Gram's house and I stood, half hanging outside, watching. What were they waiting for?

Then I heard the whistling, and I knew the tune. It was "Darling Clementine." The crow took off. Clem, I thought. That's Clem.

The other birds followed, streaking away across the pinkness of dawn. I watched till they were dots in the distance.

Where had the whistling come from? It had seemed close, but the garden outside and the street beyond were empty.

Were the birds ghosts? Was the whistler?

The room was cold. The chill was coming from the open glass case. Its sides dripped water.

I tried to think the whole thing out. Was the case a freezer? Had the birds been held there, frozen alive for all those years? When Rub-a-dub let the air in, had they come unfrozen?

I'd heard of deep-freeze experiments on people. There was even a name for it—cryo something. Bill Bedder had been a scientist. Maybe the cryo stuff was one of his newfangled ideas. Maybe he'd frozen the birds before he died. But he was dead himself now, so who had whistled? Could he

have frozen himself, too, and brought himself back? Or was he only a ghost?

I thought of them, the spook birds and the spook whistler, and for some reason I wasn't afraid anymore. They had been together in life. I knew somehow they were together again. Bill Bedder had planned it.

I closed my eyes and remembered the birds' joy as they winged their way to freedom. I remembered how they'd circled against the sky.

There was no need for the freezer case anymore. I pulled the plug and stood, listening to the silence.

EVE BUNTING has written 130 books for children, several of them award winners. Her latest book published by Albert Whitman is *The Skate Patrol.* Mrs. Bunting and her husband live in California. Of *The Spook Birds,* she says, "I have always liked spooky, creepy tales. Perhaps it is because I am Irish and once lived in a house with its own resident ghosts."

BLANCHE SIMS was born in Cleveland, Ohio, and now lives in Middletown, Connecticut. She has four grown children. She has illustrated covers and books and won several awards in fine arts. Mrs. Sims enjoys telling ghost stories to children and especially loves to draw anything that is mysterious or ghostly.